One Watermelon Seed

Celia Barker Lottridge

illustrations by Karen Patkau

Fitzhenry & Whiteside

Originally published in 1986 by Oxford University Press
First published by Fitzhenry & Whiteside in 2008

Published in Canada by Fitzhenry & Whiteside, 195 Allstate Parkway, Markham, Ontario L3R 4T8
Published in the United States by Fitzhenry & Whiteside, 311 Washington Street, Brighton, Massachusetts 02135

www.fitzhenry.ca godwit@fitzhenry.ca

10 9 8 7 6 5 4 3 2 1

Library and Archives Canada Cataloguing in Publication

Lottridge, Celia Barker
   One watermelon seed / Celia Barker Lottridge ; illustrations by Karen Patkau.

ISBN 978-1-55455-222-1

1. Counting—Juvenile literature. 2. Gardening—Juvenile literature.
I. Patkau, Karen II. Title.

QA113.L67 2012   j513.2'11   C2012-901856-2

Publisher Cataloging-in-Publication Data (U.S)

Lottridge, Celia Barker.
   One watermelon seed / Celia Barker Lottridge ; illustrations by Karen Patkau.
   [32] p. : col. photos. ; cm.

Summary: Max and Josephine plant their garden, where there are ample opportunities to count by ones. And when the crops are har-
vested, it's time to count by tens.

ISBN: 978-1-55455-222-1
1. Counting – Juvenile literature. 2. Gardening – Juvenile literature. 3. Plants – Counting – Juvenile literature. I. Patkau, Karen, Jacque-
line. II. Title.
513.211 dc23   QA113.L688 2012

Fitzhenry & Whiteside acknowledges with thanks the Canada Council for the Arts, and the Ontario Arts Council
for their support of our publishing program. We acknowledge the financial support of the Government of Canada
through the Canada Book Fund (CBF) for our publishing activities.

 Canada Council   Conseil des Arts   ONTARIO ARTS COUNCIL
for the Arts   du Canada   CONSEIL DES ARTS DE L'ONTARIO

Design by Wycliffe Smith Designs

Printed in China by Sheck Wah Tong Printing Press Ltd

In this deceptively simple counting book, Max and Josephine tend their garden. And as they plant their seeds, young readers can count along from one to ten. When the crop is ready to harvest, readers will be able to count in groups of tens while they search through the pictures for the many small animals that are hidden throughout. A concise and clever text introduces color and rhythm, while the luminous illustrations are saturated with colors that pop off the page, making counting a snap.

First published in 1986 and a staple ever since for teachers and parents of preschool children, **ONE WATERMELON SEED** is presented in a brand new edition with a bold cover and brilliant interior art.

Max and Josephine planted a garden.

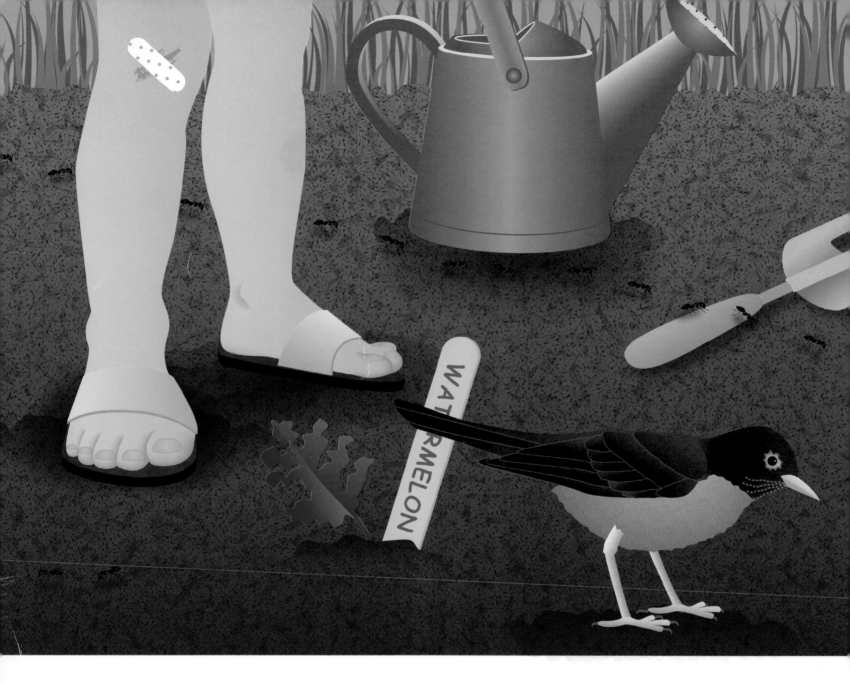

They planted one watermelon seed…and it grew.

1

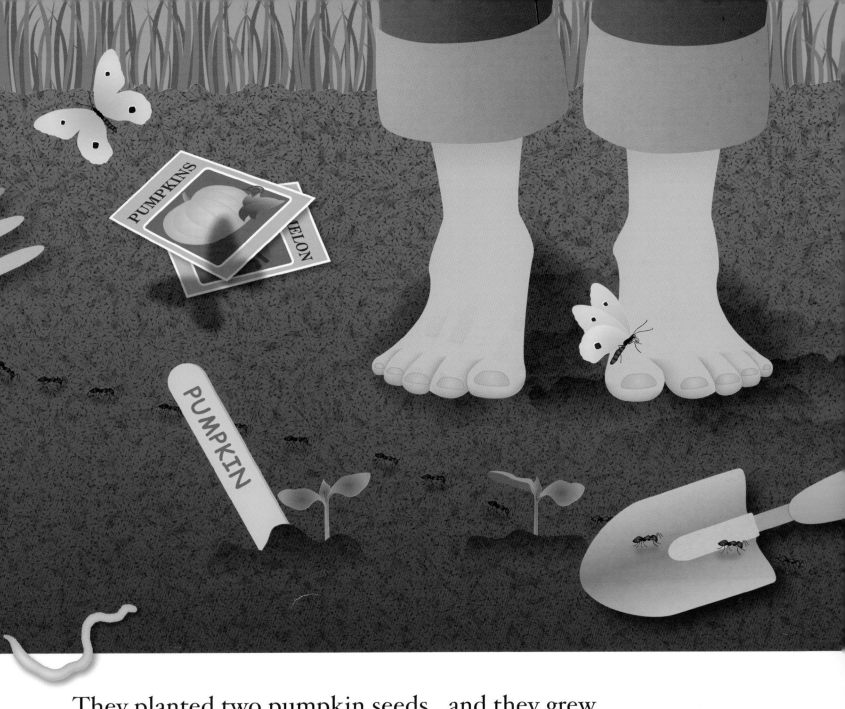

They planted two pumpkin seeds...and they grew.

1 2

Max planted three eggplants...and they grew.
1 2 **3**

Josephine planted four pepper seeds...and they grew.

1 2 **3** 4

Then she planted five tomato plants...and they grew.

1 2 **3** 4 5

Max planted six blueberry bushes...and they grew,

1 **2** **3** **4** **5** **6**

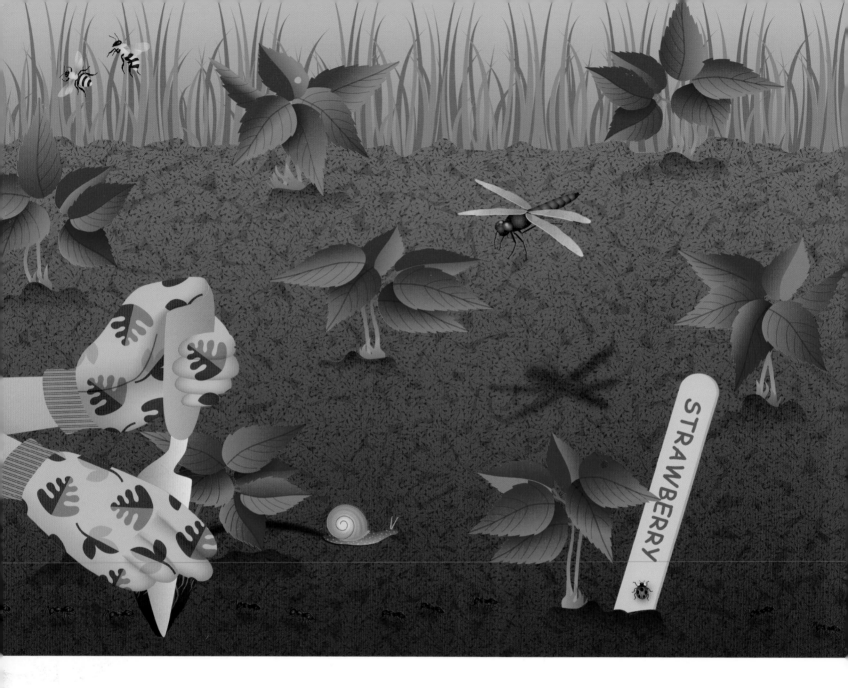

and seven strawberry plants...and they grew.

1 2 **3** 4 5 **6** 7

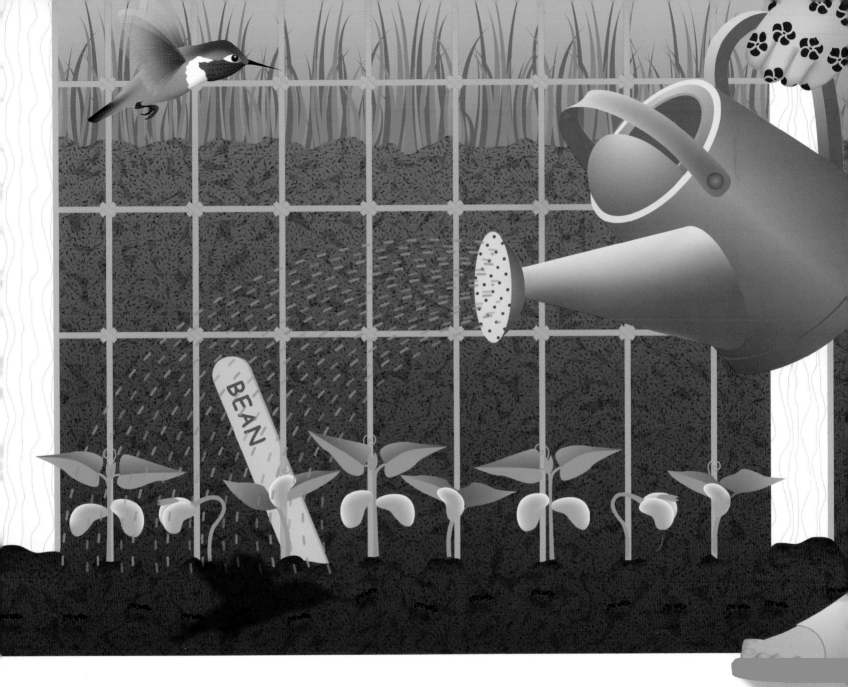

Josephine planted eight bean seeds...and they grew,

1 2 3 4 5 6 7 8

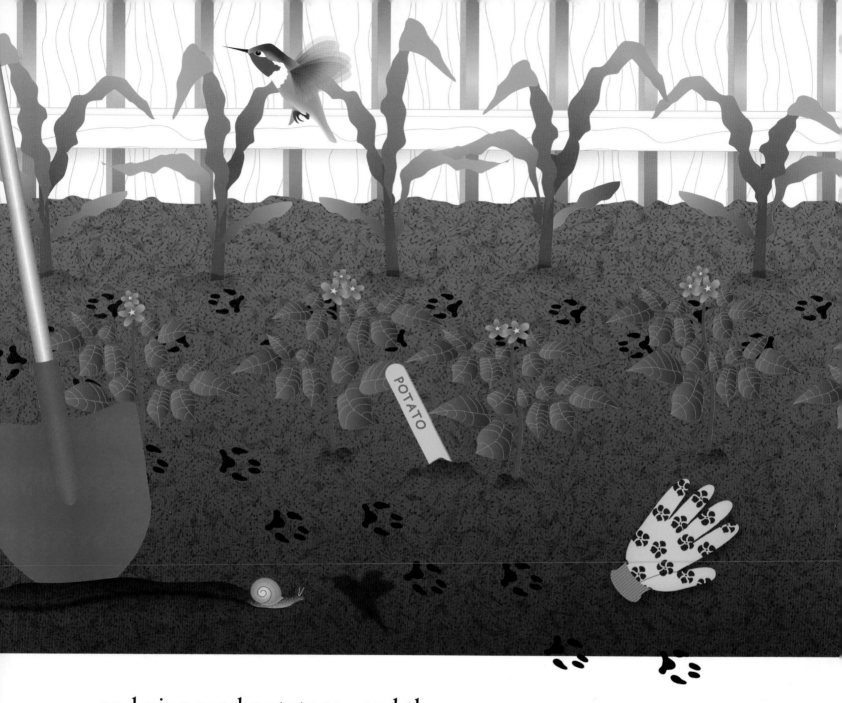

and nine seed potatoes...and they grew.
1 2 3 4 5 6 7 8 9

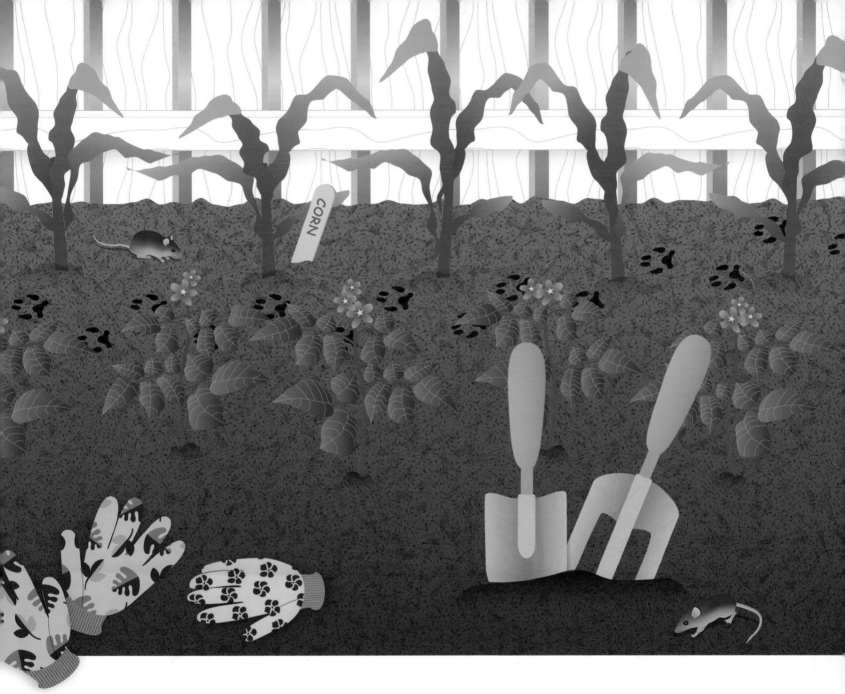

They planted ten corn seeds...and they grew.

1 2 **3** 4 5 **6** 7 **8** 9 10

The rain fell and the sun shone. The seeds and the leaves, the stalks and the vines **grew** and **grew** and **grew**.

Can you find any of these creatures in the garden?

hummingbird

fly

caterpillar

butterfly

ladybug

dragonfly

robin

mouse

earthworm

bee

ant

snail

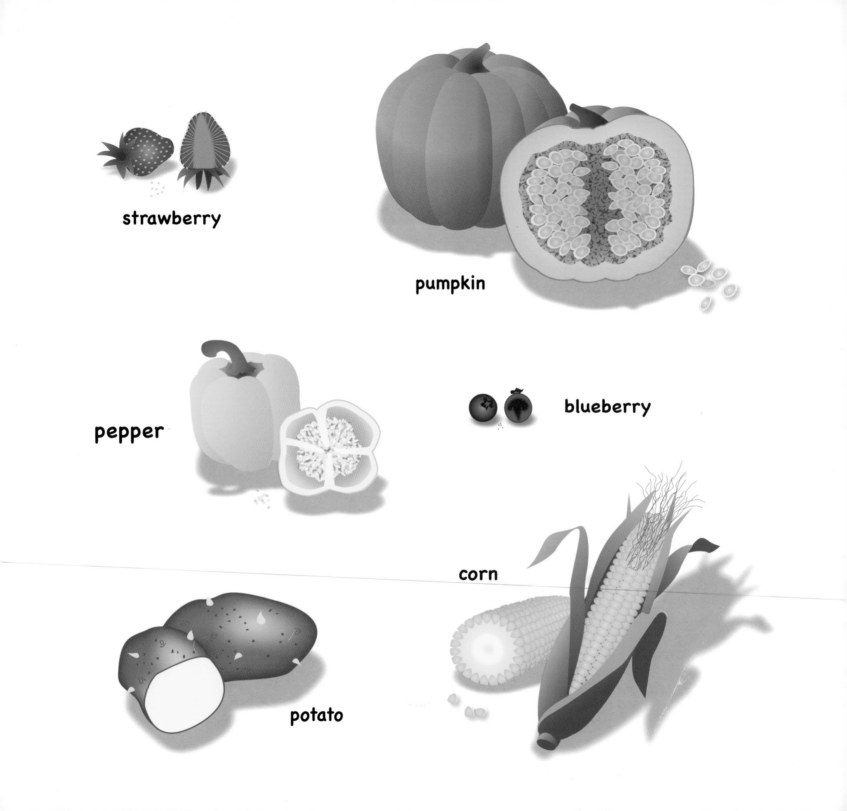

strawberry

pumpkin

pepper

blueberry

corn

potato

Look inside the garden fruits and vegetables.

watermelon

eggplant

tomato

bean

Then they turned it into 100s and 1000s of big, white crunchy puffs because that corn was

POPCORN

It was not ordinary corn. Max and Josephine saved it for cold winter nights, when the garden was covered with snow.

and they picked one hundred ears of corn.

10 20 **30** 40 50 **60** 70 **80** 90 100

Josephine dug ninety potatoes, nobby and brown,

10 20 **30** 40 50 **60** 70 **80** 90

Max picked eighty string beans, thin and crisp.

10 20 **30** 40 50 **60** 70 80

Josephine picked seventy strawberries, sweet and red.

10 20 **30** 40 50 **60** 70

and sixty blueberries, small and round.

10 20 30 40 50 60

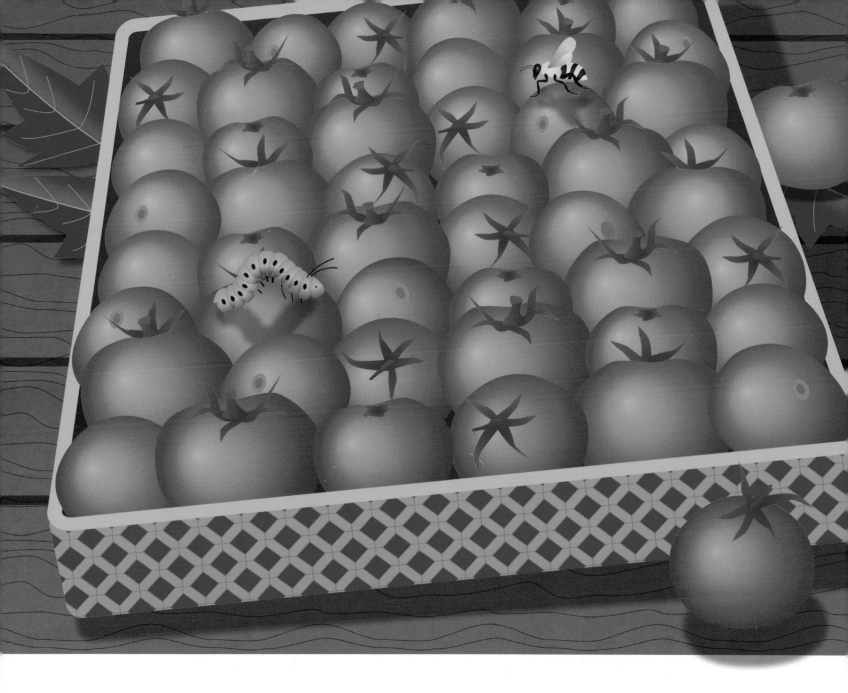

They both picked fifty tomatoes, plump and juicy,

10 20 **30** 40 50

and forty peppers, shiny yellow.
10 20 30 40

Max picked thirty eggplants, dark and purple,

10 20 **30**

and twenty pumpkins, glowing orange.

10 20

They picked ten watermelons, big and green,

10

Max and Josephine weeded and watered and waited. One day they looked at their garden and saw there was plenty to pick. So...